This book is dedicated to my beloved
mother, Michele Ann Goldman, to fulfill her
dream, and to my precious son,
Alex James Meltzer, my dream fulfilled.

You are the only ones who know what my
heart sounds like from the inside. I love you
with all that I am, and all that I will ever be.

www.mascotbooks.com

When You Lived in My Belly

For more information, please contact:
Mascot Books
620 Herndon Parkway #320
Herndon, VA 20170
info@mascotbooks.com

Library of Congress Control Number: 2019904260

CPSIA Code: PRT051A
ISBN-13: 978-1-54396-031-0

Printed in the United States

WHEN YOU LIVED IN MY BELLY

JODI MELTZER DARTER

Illustrated by Caryn King &
Jody King Camarra

When you lived in my belly during month one,
I thought being pregnant would be so much fun.
But I must admit I felt a little sick,
Sometimes I had to get to the potty real quick!
You'd just begun your journey in my tummy,
And I couldn't wait to be your Mummy.

When you lived in my belly during month two,

I was already amazed by you.

I started to snack on **so much food,**

Except when my belly got in a strange mood.

The doctor called you a fetus,

You doubled in size and I couldn't believe it!

When you lived in my belly during month three,

My darling baby, you were meant to be.

My belly got bigger and harder to hide,

I was happy to tell people you were living inside.

You had arms, hands, fingers, feet, and toes,

You could even make your fists open and close.

When you lived in my belly during month four,
You were ready to show off like you owned the dance floor.
I saw you on an ultrasound and it **filled me with joy**,
I could even find out if you were a girl or a boy.
Your eyelids, eyebrows, and eyelashes were formed,
You made silly faces, stretched, and yawned.

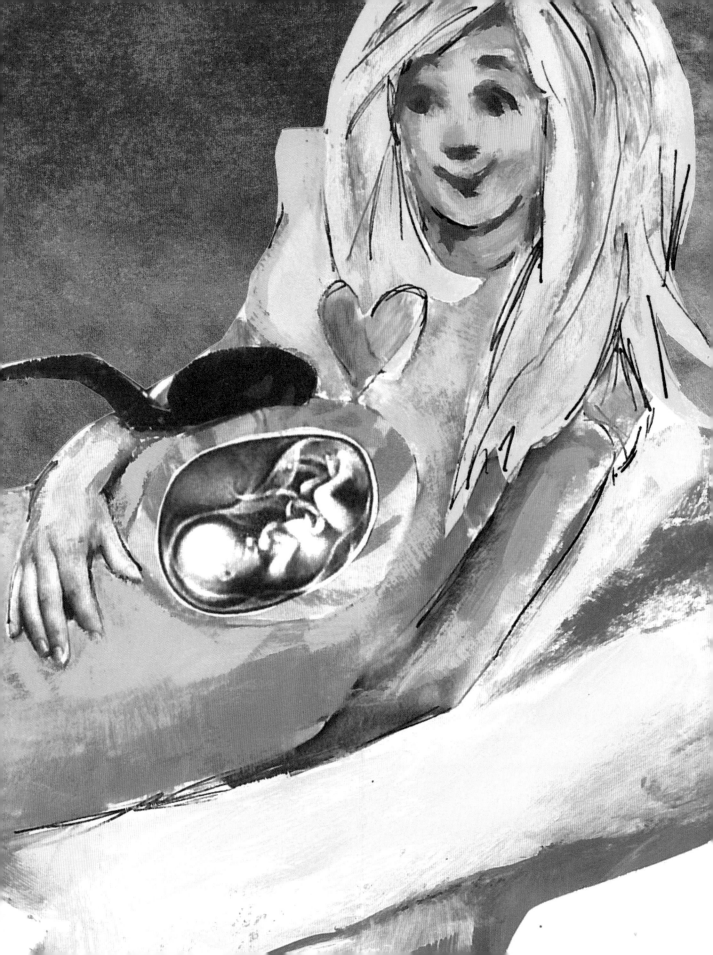

When you lived in my belly during month five,
Your constant movement made me **feel alive.**
You flipped and tumbled—wow, were you good,
You **bounced around** like a gymnast would!
You spent each day getting lots of exercise,
Growing big, strong muscles by moving your thighs.

When you lived in my belly during month six,
You added **hiccups** to your bag of tricks.
I kept thinking about how I'd decorate your room,
Knowing you would arrive pretty soon.
By now you were able to open your eyes,
Seeing for the first time must have been **a surprise.**

When you lived in my belly during month seven,

Some nights you kept me awake past eleven!

I stayed up late reading my pregnancy book,

And craved certain foods I just had to cook.

You could hear clearly and responded to sound,

You listened to music and danced around.

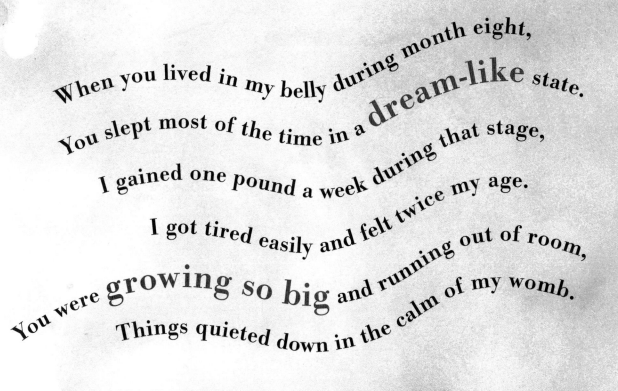

When you lived in my belly during month eight,
You slept most of the time in a dream-like state.
I gained one pound a week during that stage,
I got tired easily and felt twice my age.
You were growing so big and running out of room,
Things quieted down in the calm of my womb.

When you lived in my belly and it was finally month nine,
I couldn't wait to kiss you, **beautiful baby** of mine.
Sleeping, bending over, even walking was hard,
I worried about you coming and was always on guard.
You made your way toward the birth canal,
Ready to **meet Mommy** someway, somehow.

When you left my belly on the day you were born,

You didn't tell me you were coming, I wasn't forewarned.

I had to be as patient as I could possibly be,

And work hard until you could come meet me.

When you entered the world and started to cry,

You were placed on my chest with a sweet little sigh.

When you look at my belly even today,

Remember it was once your special place to stay.

That time we spent together was beyond compare,

We were part of a **miracle** only us two could share.

I am so grateful you grew close to my heart,

And I always loved you right from the start.

WHEN YOU LIVED IN MY BELLY...

_____

_____

_____

_____

_____

_____

_____

_____

_____

_____

_____

_____

_____

_____

_____

_____

_____

Acknowledgments

First, I must profess my adoration for my brilliant, hilarious, and infinitely patient husband, Mike Darter, whose fingerprints are all over this book. Thank you for being my favorite second reader, for dissecting and debating every word, and for believing in my vision. Your endless love always makes me feel like the sun shines directly on my face. Lava you pinf.

My best friend since kindergarten, Jody King Camarra, worked tirelessly between school drop-offs, pick-ups, and PTA meetings to bring this book to life. I am forever grateful for your forty years of friendship and for all of the exquisite illustrations, revisions, and iterations. I will miss our late-night book brainstorming sessions, but look forward to the next chapter. I love you.

Caryn King (CK)—I admire your talent, creativity, expertise, and insight. You got us across the finish line with finesse.

Jill Gurfinkel, thank you for being you. You have never given up on me, and I love you for it. Sister stars.

I appreciate your thoughtful edits, Heidi Sadler, all of those years ago.

To my bonus children, Ashley Rose Meltzer and Jacob Reese Darter, thank you for giving me another perspective on parenting and for trusting me with your hearts. I will always hold them close to mine.

Finally, thank you, Alex James, for giving me the greatest gift of being your mom. You are sweet, feisty, intelligent, talented, handsome, inquisitive, compassionate, loving, and loyal...a good friend to others and an even better son to me. Your silly antics, quick wit, and flawless dance moves always inspire me to join in on your fun. Keep being you, my sonshine, and you will forever make me proud. I love you beyond measure, and I will never forget what it was like when you lived in my belly.